Produced by The Creative Spark
San Clemente, California

Illustrated by Yakovetic Productions

Printed in the United States of America.

ISBN 0-7172-8381-X

Grolier Books is a division of Grolier Enterprises, Inc.

Cheer Up, Sebastian

The deep blue sea around the Little Mermaid's island was calm, but Sebastian the crab was not. He was having a bad day. Everything was going wrong. He hadn't slept a wink, and already that morning he'd broken his toothbrush and gotten some seamoss stuck in his claw. *Maybe*, he thought to himself, *I'll feel better if I go see Ariel.*

"Oh, Sebastian! You
look terrible!" the Little
Mermaid said when she saw her little friend.

"I feel terrible," replied Sebastian. "If one more bad
thing happens to me today I'll—"

But before he could finish what he was saying, a teacup fell from one
of the nooks in Ariel's grotto and landed on his head.

Ariel gently lifted the teacup off her friend. "That does it!" Sebastian bellowed. "Now I'm really angry!"

"Oh, Sebastian," Ariel said as she patted the bump on his head, "when you're having a bad day, the best thing to do is just relax and take it easy. Getting angry will only make things worse."

"Who told you such nonsense?" snapped the little crab.

"You did," Ariel laughed.

"Oh," said Sebastian, embarrassed by his forgetfulness. "Then it must be true."

And so Sebastian left Ariel's grotto, found a good book to read, and went up to the inviting beach. "This is much better," he said as he sat down. "I should take my own advice more often."

But just as he was getting comfortable, the sunlight was blocked by a huge shadow passing overhead. It was Scuttle the seagull, and he was heading straight for Sebastian!

"Gangway!" cried the clumsy bird. "Abandon beach!" But it was too late. Scuttle swooped in low, and both the seagull and the tiny crab went tumbling across the sand. "Another perfect landing," Scuttle said proudly.

"Scuttle, you birdbrain," howled Sebastian, "you've ruined my sunbathing!"

"Really?" said Scuttle. "If you ask me, you've been out in the sun long enough. Look at how red you are!"

"I didn't ask you—and I'm always this red!" Sebastian shouted as he picked up his book. "I'm a crab!"

"You sure are," Scuttle mumbled as Sebastian stalked away.

Sebastian searched for a quiet place under the sea to spend the rest of the day. Just as he settled on a nice big rock, Flounder the fish and his twin sister, Sandy, swam by. "Hi, Sebastian!" they called out. "Want to play hide-and-seek with us?"

"No, thank you," replied Sebastian. "I'm going to stay right here on this rock until my bad day is over. I'm not moving an inch!"

"But Sebastian—" Sandy started to say, pointing beneath the crab.

"Not another word," the crab commanded. "I'm not moving."

Suddenly, the rock moved! It wasn't a rock after all, it was a giant sea turtle!

Sebastian bumped—UMPH!—and bounced—OOF!—to the ocean floor. "Are you all right?" Sandy asked.

"Go away!" the little crab snapped at them. "Leave me alone! I'm having a terrible day!"

"What a crabby crab," Flounder said to his sister as they swam away. "Let's go visit Scales instead."

Scales was a friendly dragon who lived in a wonderful cave that twisted and turned and ran deep into the ground. He loved to play marbles and bake muffins and sing silly songs.

Flounder and Sandy told Scales about the bad day Sebastian was having, and how grumpy he was.

"I have just the thing to cheer him up," the dragon replied. "I made a batch of seaberry muffins this morning. They're Sebastian's favorite."

Before going to see Sebastian, Scales cleaned up his kitchen and put away his baking things. Scales liked everything in its place.

"That's funny," he said. "One of my marbles is missing."

Meanwhile, Sebastian decided to visit his lovely tidepool garden. The seeds he had planted were not sprouting yet, but he loved the peace and quiet all the same. *Maybe my garden will help me relax and feel better*, Sebastian thought. And soon he was taking a nice little nap among the mussels and barnacles.

"There you are!" shouted Scales, waking the crab with a start. "I thought I'd find you here!"

"Oh, Scales, couldn't you see I was sleeping?" Sebastian scowled.

"I'm sorry," said Scales. "But I heard you were having a bad day, so I brought you some seaberry muffins."

"Muffins!" Sebastian cried. "Why didn't you say so?" He couldn't wait to munch on his favorite dessert.

Sebastian opened his mouth. CRUNCH! He bit down on something hard—it was Scales's missing marble. "Aaagh!" Sebastian cried. "My tooth!"

"My marble!" said Scales. "I wondered what happened to it."

Sebastian was furious. "Leave me alone!" he grumbled. "Just go away before you make things worse!"

"Gee, Sebastian," Scales said, "I was only trying to help."

"I SAID GO AWAY!" the little crab yelled. And so, with a tear in his eye, Scales paddled back to the lagoon and his cave.

Yelling at Scales made Sebastian feel even worse. After all, Scales just wanted to cheer him up. That's all any of his friends had meant to do. *I'm having a bad day*, Sebastian thought, *and I took it out on them.*

"This is the worst day of my life," Sebastian said to the mussels and barnacles. "I think I just lost all my friends."

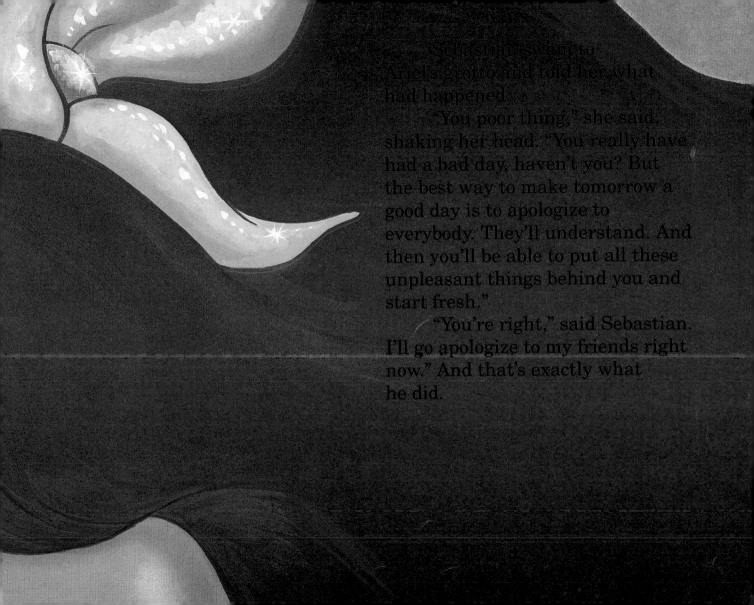

Sebastian swam to Ariel's grotto and told her what had happened.

"You poor thing," she said, shaking her head. "You really have had a bad day, haven't you? But the best way to make tomorrow a good day is to apologize to everybody. They'll understand. And then you'll be able to put all these unpleasant things behind you and start fresh."

"You're right," said Sebastian. "I'll go apologize to my friends right now." And that's exactly what he did.

The next day, Ariel found Scales and Sebastian working together in the crab's garden. Flounder, Sandy, and even Scuttle, were there.

"Look, Ariel," Sebastian beamed, "my garden is starting to grow! And best of all, Scales and Flounder and Sandy and Scuttle are helping me plant some more seeds. They're not angry at me, and we're all still friends."

"That's wonderful!" replied the Little Mermaid. "You see? Bad days never last, but good friends are forever."